To Baby Jack - The Best x
G.B.

To my parents,
who should have been here to see this book;
and to very best Baby . . . Henry!
A.S.

This paperback edition first published in 2014 by Andersen Press Ltd.
First published in Great Britain in 2013 by Andersen Press Ltd., 20 Vauxhall Bridge Road, London SW1V 2SA.
Published in Australia by Random House Australia Pty., Level 3, 100 Pacific Highway, North Sydney, NSW 2060.
Text copyright © Anthea Simmons, 2013. Illustration copyright © Georgie Birkett, 2013
The rights of Anthea Simmons and Georgie Birkett to be identified as the author and illustrator
of this work have been asserted by them in accordance with the Copyright, Designs and Patents Act, 1988.
All rights reserved. Colour separated in Switzerland by Photolitho AG, Zürich.
Printed and bound in Malaysia by Tien Wah Press.
Georgie Birkett has used pencil and acrylics in this book.

10   9   8   7   6   5   4   3   2   1

British Library Cataloguing in Publication Data available.

ISBN 978 1 78344 044 3

This book has been printed on acid-free paper

THE BEST, BEST BABY!

ANTHEA SIMMONS   GEORGIE BIRKETT

ANDERSEN PRESS

My little brother's still pretty new
And there's still lots of stuff
that he can't do.

He can't really run

And he can't climb trees!

He can't say "thank you"
And he can't say "please"!

He can't dress himself.
He can't choose his clothes!

He can't brush his teeth

And he can't blow his nose!

He can't draw a picture

But he CAN make a mess
And he can throw food

And he can stick his
tongue out
And be very rude!

And he can get very dirty

YAAA

AAAAAH!

And he can scream and shout.

And "Me!"

and "cake"

and "out!"

He can get up too early.
He can keep me awake.

He can break my toys sometimes
(Mum says it's by mistake).

And when I'm getting grumpy
And wish he wasn't there

He smiles his special baby smile

And tugs on my hair.

And stares at my face.

He holds on tightly to my hand

And that's when I know that

no-one can take his place.

And even though there's lots of stuff
That makes me cross or sad.

He's still the best, BEST baby brother

That a sister ever had.

Also available:

Paperback: 9781849392204
Board book: 9781849392952

Board book: 9781783440412